John Hillhouse

The Annunciation: A Poem

John Hillhouse

The Annunciation: A Poem

ISBN/EAN: 9783742860323

Manufactured in Europe, USA, Canada, Australia, Japa

Cover: Foto ©Andreas Hilbeck / pixelio.de

Manufactured and distributed by brebook publishing software
(www.brebook.com)

John Hillhouse

The Annunciation: A Poem

THE ANNUNCIATION.

A POEM.

BY

JOHN HILLHOUSE.

Ἰδοὺ ἡ παρθένος ἐν γαστρὶ λήψεται, καὶ τέξεται υἱόν.
—Is. vii. 14.

WITH ILLUSTRATIONS

FROM ORIGINAL DESIGNS BY

THE AUTHOR.

NEW YORK:
POTT & AMERY, 5 & 13 COOPER UNION.
1868.

TO THOSE TO WHOM,—

IN THESE DAYS WHEN THE LIGHT AND THE SENSATIONAL ARE IN SUCH EAGER DEMAND,—

*A moderate Indulgence in the Serious will afford a
pleasurable variety,*

THIS LITTLE BOOK,

ON A SUBJECT OF THE DEEPEST INTEREST AND IMPORTANCE,

IS HUMBLY AND HOPEFULLY

Inscribed.

Nihil quod promoveat scriptor, vel mutare vel movere poterit sententiam populi, de ejus meritis quod populari acumini committitur.

New York, June, 1868.

The Holy Ghost shall come upon thee, and the power of the Highest shall overshadow thee: therefore also that holy thing which shall be born of thee shall be called the Son of God.

—St. Luke I. 35.

THE ANNUNCIATION.

Hail, thou that art highly favoured, the Lord is with thee: blessed art thou among women!—St. Luke, I. 28.

FROM Heaven's resplendent portals issuing,

Whose pearly heights, bath'd in refulgent light,

Catch the first glow of the celestial morn,

Stood Gabriel on the brink, the mighty brink

That wide o'erlooks the illimitable bounds,

Ethereal, azure, pure, empyreal :—

For now the fullness of the time had come,

That, manifest in flesh, of Virgin born

The Eternal Word should be; his precious Life

The ransom high to pay for man's redemption ;

And him the Almighty Father summoning,

Had high commission given, on rapid wing

To the holy man the tidings glad to bear,

Who, in the order of his priestly course

Minister'd even then before the Lord,

And made his prayer, that God his promis'd
    word

Would soon fulfill and bless his chosen race.—

Divine in symmetry the Angel stood,

With half-expanded wings, pois'd o'er th' abyss;

His glittering vestments shining as the sun,

And golden zone circling his comely waist:

A moment stood, his brow illustrious fair,

Gleaming with ardor of his high intent;

Scanning with spirit's far regard the way

'Mong countless systems, sphere on sphere in-
    volv'd

In endless order, far through infinite space

To this terrene : not that it unknown was,

Though trackless all, whose only varying
    guides

The rolling worlds ; for well know heavenly
    minds

Each planet place to assign, and wand'ring star ;

Whether in opposition they, or like

Degree in zodiac hold, or are occult,

Or in immersion set : and oft before

Ambassador on mission of import,

He had sought earth's sacred places. Thus he
    stood ;

When, forth-spreading wide his ample wings,

Bath'd in the purple glow of heavenly light,

As leaps the lightning from the rifted cloud,

And casts its flashing glance athwart the
    heavens,

So, vaulting from his stand the fearless Angel

Swift darted through the vast ethereal depths,

Steering his rapid flight, with spirit's instinct

Rare, through wild'ring ocean of expanse.

Fell sweet, fell grateful on his charmèd sense,

In numbers soft of heavenly harmony,

From lute and harp and voice of Cherubim,

Rising Heaven's jasper battlements above,

The glorious anthem of Messiah's love :

As parting her precincts, he veers his flight,

With unabated speed, toward the shores

Of time : till Heaven delighted heard thro' all

Her courts, and sang with answering tongue his

   praise.

Full soon, like meteor darting swift, he cross'd

That utmost orb whose planet's place and path

Sure science fix'd before its light descry'd,

And held his course, nor folded once his wing,

Till, as the aged priest from prayer arose,

Through clouds of fragrant incense, golden fring'd,
He stood, in splendor to his sight reveal'd.

Through clouds of fragrant incense, golden
    fring'd,
He stood, in splendor to his sight reveal'd.

Stood, full confess'd in glittering robes of
    light,
The angel presence, to the trembling priest;
With rev'rent awe involuntary mov'd :
Supernal luster from his beauteous brow
Irradiating bright; his golden locks
Thrown back, down flowing, tremulous of light,
And o'er his head a circling glory hung :
Glow his fair cheeks with ardor of his zeal,
And all his state momentous embassy
Imports, as thus encouraging he speaks :
    Fear not : thy prayer is heard; and I, to
        give
Assurance, am to thee of purpose sent.
Attend my word : From thee a son shall spring,

Harbinger of Messias, Prince of Peace;
Whom in Elijah's power he shall precede,
With spirit's unction fill'd.   Joy shalt thou
    have
And gladness at his birth ; whose voice, aloud,
Persuasive shall proclaim the King's advance
Triumphant.—When the wondering priest, in
    doubt,
To thought oblivious of Omnipotence :
    Wondrous the plan thou deign'st to me
    unfold,
Celestial Messenger! whose marvelous words,
As beauty of whose countenance benign,
Extraction not of earth betok'neth clear.
Unworthy both to hear, as in myself
Fulfillment unexpected to receive,
Of the bless'd Promise, long'd for, long delay'd.
Seeing how far my race of life is run,

Safe by GOD carry'd, ev'n to these hoar hairs,

And that my wife is old and strick'n in years,

Grant me a sign, whereby I know this thing,

And e'en 'gainst hope, yet still in hope believe.

Whom, answering, thus the Seraph made
reply:—

Faithful in heart, though weak in faith, a sign

Thou seekest, to confirm thy slow belief:

Know, then, that Gabriel I, who trusting stand

In GOD's eternal presence, and am sent,

These tidings, at which angels most rejoice,

To bear to thee, high favor'd of the LORD.

Behold, thou shalt be dumb; nor word shalt
speak,

Until the day these things be all perform'd;

Because my truthful word thou'st not believ'd.

So vanish'd, and rewing'd his joyful flight

Up to his native Heaven. Full soon delights

His view her gorgeous towers, her battlements,
With millions crown'd of glitt'ring 'habitants,
Him beck'ning fond, hailing with loud acclaim,
Waving their shining wings in welcome glad:
Full soon breaks on his ear her minstrelsy
From golden harps by angel fingers swept:
There joy'd to join anew the swelling flood
Symphonious, of soft accordant sounds;
There joy'd to dwell, where fruits immortal
    grow,
And living streams from spiritual fountains flow;
Where is no light of sun, of grief no sting,
But God the light, and joy's perpetual spring.

His ministration ended, now retir'd,
Thoughtful and deep impress'd, the holy man
To Hebron, in Judea's mount, his home;
Where, to devotion given, and patient thought

Of GOD's mysterious, moving providence,

Whose hand invisible had in silence seal'd

The organs of his utt'rance, liv'd retir'd.

And came to pass the Angel's truthful word.

His saintly wife,—of priestly Aaron's race,

Upright in heart, and righteous before GOD

The tide of gladness filling all her soul;

Who, all her life prolong'd, in hope had walk'd;

Grateful for tender dealings of the LORD,

Who, pitying her affliction, had remov'd

Her sad reproach,—in secret from the world

Withdrew, and gave to contemplation calm,

To prayer, to praise, to self-abasement just,

Her expectant days of anxious solitude.

Now fairest Day-spring, blushing bride of

morn,

Cloth'd in chaste garments, from the nuptial East

Rejoicing came, and with her rosy hand
Unrob'd the sleeping Earth, in dusk attire.
Fair shone her smile on stern Judea's hills,
Fair on her fruitful vales; those hills, those vales,
With riches dropping of their fragrant load;
Where every mountain tribute paid to toil;
High on whose rocky breasts the clinging vine
Its lively juice, its oil, the olive drank;—
Once a blest heritage: wasted now and lone:
Sad desolation brooding over all.
Save when the Christian pilgrim, led by love,
With consecrated feet its sacred vales
Lingers among; or on its holy heights
Lives with the past, and feasts his longing eyes
Delighted, where feasted oft his heart before,—
Only the prowling Bedouin is seen;
His shout alone disturbs the death-like spell,
Where ancient Solitude in gloomy state,

Reigns o'er a widow'd, sad, unpeopl'd realm.

. Eastward, by Kedron's course toward the sea,

Rose many a hoary top, with verdant belt

Encircl'd; or bath'd in crimson blush of dawn,

Or shadow'd dark; range intersecting range:

And many a city from commanding height

Look'd down: here, Aphek, strong and tried
    in war,

Bar'd her gray walls; there stately Nebschan
    rose;

And priestly Alemeth: while, Jordan past,

Pisgah and Nebo, chief of Abarim,—

High seats of Chemosh, Moab's idol god,

Where Pethor's prophet, by enchantment sought

The LORD to win, and Israel bless'd constrain'd;

Regarding base reward of sordid gain,—

Rear'd their bare forheads to the azure vault:

And northward, Gilead, canopy'd in oak,

And leafy Bashan's waving hills embrac'd.

Fresh odors from the dewy fields arose,
And balmy breath of morn, by nightly hands
Perfum'd with spicy treasures from the isles,
And distant Meroë, distill'd its sweets:
Saba her tribute paid of frankincense;
And myrrh, from Astabora's borders brought
And Shendi's aromatic vales, with nard
From Yemen's sunny shores commingl'd.   Now
The wakeful birds wafted their carol'd chant
Of praise, trusting, to Him whose unseen hand
Their daily fare provides; and patient flocks,
From fold releas'd, went gamb'ling forth, their
        day,
The simple pattern of their simple lives,
Or on the verdant slopes to spend, or by
The stream, browsing the tender grasses sweet;
Or, unconcern'd for life's vicissitudes,

And all beside, save nature's wants so few,
So simple, measur'd right, reposing meek.

Join'd in the general matin hymn, that
burst
Rapturous, from golden hill and dewy field;
From odorous sweets, and warbling bird, and
flock,—
For these have voices all, His love to own,
Tho' favor'd man so oft ungrateful prove :—
Join'd with more grateful praise, because en-
dued
With reason's power, the tender love to trace
In every gift of kind beneficence,
Two beings, who, the early morning hour
Surpris'd, tow'rd Kirjath Arba journeying.
Female and male they were. He, prime in
years,

Where judgment and discretion guide : she,
    where
The virginal cheek of timid maidenhood,
With blush more deep suffus'd, more mantling
    soft,
Just into ripeness mellows, ere begins
The charm, the grace subdu'd, of womanhood.
His brow expansive was with wisdom stamp'd ;
And goodness, gently pleading from his eye,
From all his mien humility, bespoke
Of mind and heart the true nobility.
She beside him walk'd ; her garb like his
Betok'ning humble state. Of feebler sex,
Submission, like a veil cloth'd and adorn'd :
Yet in her gesture, gait, and graceful port,
A something shone superior forth, that told
Of proud descent, no poverty could hide,
Or homely garb disguise. He look'd on her

Solicitous, with fond regard; with love
And gentle sweetness mingl'd, she on him.
Since our first mother 'mid the countless forms
Of beauty inexpressible, herself
Most beauteous, most attractive fair, her charms
Unfolded on that bridal morn, when man
First claim'd her in espousals sweet, and forth
She walk'd in admiring Paradise, forth from
Creative Wisdom's matchless hand, of earth
The masterpiece; peerless 'mong all its works;
The fairest she. She saw in him, his love,
His worth, his tenderness and fostering care,
Her life's protector, life's companion dear.
He, in her gentleness, confiding heart,
Her wakeful sympathies, her mind serene,
And some mysterious grace that seem'd to
    link
Her being with divinity,—his joy,

His pride; the pledge of sacred confidence;
Of love's sweet converse down the walks of life.

Thus, as they onward held their way, with
    hearts
To love's suggestions soft, beating response,
Varied discourse arose : each incident,
Each changing scene, unmark'd of some, the
    past
To mind recalling, or impressing new;
And nature's charms seductive, manifold,
Communion prompting : but chief the thoughts
    that rose
For Zion's sadness.
                Pleasant this early hour,—
Thus she began,—to walk abroad and meet
The morn advancing from the hills, to kiss
With rosy lips the new-awaken'd earth;

And raise, with nature's voice unanimous,

The soul's pure meed of adoration due

To Him, Creator wise, who all upholds,

Good, who all things supplies.   Whom answer-

    ing, her

Companion :—

        True, Mary belov'd, thy words ;

As ever, heavenward bent, on grateful wings.

When every sense is clear, the frame by sleep

Invigorated, may we best approach

With fitting praise the Mercy-seat ; best feel,

Then best confess, how much our GOD we

    owe,

Unable to repay the least.   This air

Laden with grateful scents ; these rolling fields

With sweetest grasses grown ; this harmony

Of birds ; this landscape fair ; the rising day

All life with light and warmth invigorating ;

Each flower of tender hue; each slender blade;
All do proclaim His hand, and call to praise.

　Much do we owe His care,—she fond
　　replied,—
Who prosper'd hath so well our way, and given
In many forms assurance of His love.
Long hath our journey been, yet seeming short,
So sweet with thee the interchange of thought
Hath serv'd the way to lighten and beguile.

　When he again:—None who His goodness
　　trust
May doubt His favor.　Oft, when we have
　　walk'd
On Nazareth's pleasant hills, or by her fount;
Or sought retirement in her vale embower'd,
At quiet hour, in that lov'd spot where we
Our mutual hearts confess'd, and lov'd the
　　more

But see, where bath'd in light, the holy tow'rs
Of dear Jerusalem resplendent shine!

Confessing; have I own'd, with reason just,

The debt of gratitude to that kind Power,

Who all our varied steps in life hath led;

From every danger found escape; in all

The needs that spring of poverty brought glad

Relief. Above all, grateful for thyself;

For want with thee is wealth, and labor light;

Without thee, riches were but penury.

Frequent do I recall those memories,—

The simple handmaid of the LORD;—who have

Abundant witness, in how kind regard

He hath remember'd of my low estate.—

But see, where bath'd in light, the holy towers

Of dear Jerusalem resplendent shine!

Her bow'd and stricken form in glory rob'd,

As if in mockery of her grief! for how

Can she rejoice? how lay aside her weeds

While stays her sad reproach? her children
    spoil'd;
Her beauteous, holy heritage defil'd
By Gentile sway: Ah, soon shall Zion hope
To lift again her head so. low abas'd!
Full soon to sing anew her songs of joy!

    Soon may she hope! Thus ever, dearest,
      pray.

Alas! for her transgression it is come,
The LORD his favor'd vine hath left a prey
To ruthless spoilers' hand. When Israel sought
His will, and bow'd submissive to His yoke,
He nourish'd her with tend'rest care; her wild
Luxuriance train'd or prun'd away, and hedg'd
Her borders round about with love: He
    watch'd
Her budding forth and bloom, and how she
    grew,

And spread her branches wide, with rich return

Of pleasant fruit; that nations came from far

To see the goodly vine our GOD had planted.

But when she chang'd her love, and gave her
    heart

To idols, and would none of his reproofs,

But all his tender yearnings, loving pleas,

With bitter scorn rejected and despis'd;

Then, mercy slighted, patience wearied quite,

He withdrew his care, and gave this precious
    vine,

The object of his love, to be a spoil;

That all who pass'd might pluck it, and inquire,

If this the goodly vine the LORD hath set?

O, not long be the day remov'd, ere He

Shall come, our nation's great Deliverer!

Who, as the wise affirm, should now appear.

But there is Rama's ancient ruin still,

And sacred oaks; reminding we draw nigh
To Bethlehem, the city of thy sires;
'Mong all our chief, the chosen of thy love;
Where some enchantment ever seems to bind
Thy heart.   And sure her comely towers in fair ·
Proportions rise, and fair her prospect 'round.
Let us descend, ere enter'd, to the vale,
And slake our thirst at that refreshing spring
Thy father David lov'd so well to drink.

How much do I, descended daughter, love
To dwell upon that story of his wrong!
When weary, fainting and athirst, by Saul
Pursu'd, high in Adullam cave he lay,
And there bethought him of that well so sweet,
Where oft in youth he drank, and oft his flocks,
And whose delicious, cooling draught he lov'd,
And thirsted so to taste; from which, those
        three,

Eleazar, Shummah, and the Eznite drew;
With matchless valor, thro' the Philistine host
Breaking, that lay encamp'd at Rephaim.
    With cheerful converse thus, their toilsome
      path
Enlivening, they hastened on their way.

    How little knows the heart, the good that
      waits!
How little she, in holy calm absorb'd,
Where pass'd her expectant days of solitude,
The sacred joys those hastening footsteps bring!
She, deep impress'd with sense of mercies kind
In her behalf, so signal mark'd of heaven;
With solemn sense of the surprising love
That her had chosen to so blest estate,
Unhop'd, unlook'd for, unsolicited,
The favor'd mother to become ere long

Of the predicted Harbinger, whose feet

So long ago had turned life's summit hoar,

Journeying toward the vale of years; from
world

And worldly contact kept herself withdrawn;

The better thus of heavenly things to clear

Her view; her soul from sensual delights

That wound, preserve; that in the calm com-
pose

Of sacred solitude, naught might disturb

The peaceful sessions of her holy thoughts;

Naught mar with slightest stain, the tender
germ

Impressible, of infant being, soon

His Saviour King to herald to the world.

Thus, while the queen of night in monthly
round,

Five times in syzygy her silver disk

Oppos'd, she sought seclusion : finding grace
Meanwhile, and comfort with her saintly
    spouse,
The holy records searching, in the things
Reveal'd touching the promis'd Seed. A priest
Of GOD, experienc'd long, his learning much
Her feebler powers assisted ; and though
    smit
For incredulity with loss of speech,
His silent witness, more than choicest words,
Pleaded the righteous GOD, and sinful man
Still justified through sacrificial blood.
In sacred duties thus her days she pass'd ;
And not without the fruits in rich return
Of godliness : love, gentleness, joy, peace.

As thus, upon a day she thoughtful sat,
And from the open casement, vine-embower'd,

Thro' which the cooling airs play'd soft, look'd
> forth
On the quiet scene, that in her spirit's calm
An answering chord harmonious found; while
> pale
Crepúscule crept on lingering steps of light;
Much she reflected on the past; much wish'd
The veil to lift mysterious, that hung
Inscrutable, before futurity;
And wonder'd much, of Israel's daughters, who,
More highly bless'd than she, the mighty
> Prince
Should bear, whose Forerunner, her promis'd
> son.
A Virgin shall conceive!   Amazing truth!
Above, beyond strict nature's constant laws;
And hence, the work of Hand omnipotent.
Hard to believe; but wrought in power of God:

As thus she spoke, involuntary moved,
Sudden, a gentle voice beside her;—Hail!

To comprehend, vain task: in faith await.

Of David's line the child; in Bethlehem born.

Are Bethlehem's daughters honor'd thus to be?

Does she yet live? may I behold her yet,

Before my earthly term is closed, now soon?

O, with what tender yearning would my heart,

If so my GOD this favor would bestow,

Rejoice, to see the Mother of my LORD!

    As thus she spoke, involuntary mov'd,

Sudden, a gentle voice beside her:—Hail!

Cousin, all hail! Peace be to thee and thine!

Behold, immediate, an ecstasy

Of transport all divine the matron aged

Illumin'd and possess'd. In rapt surprise:—

    Whence,—she exclaimed,—whence, Mary, this

        to me?

That, even while I made my fervent prayer,

The Mother of my Lord, indeed, should come?

Bless'd among women thou! and bless'd the
    fruit
That thou shalt bear! For, lo! as soon as fell
Thy friendly salutation on mine ears,
The babe, inspir'd, leaped in my womb for joy!
Blessèd art thou, who faithful hast believ'd;
For He who promis'd hath, will sure perform.

    And Mary said :—My soul doth magnify
The LORD : my spirit hath rejoic'd in GOD
My Saviour : for He hath regardful been
Of me, and of my low estate : Behold,
Henceforth, all nations shall me Blessèd call ;
For He that mighty is, great things hath done
To me: Holy His Name! His mercy comes
To Israël, in remembrance of His word.

    To whom Elizabeth thus:—Joy fills my
    soul
Unbounded ; bliss unclouded my rapt spirit

Swells : joy, for that thou, my near of kin,

Art chosen of the LORD ; bliss, for the hope

Made sure.　Thrice Blessèd be thou call'd, in
　　whom

GOD's favoring grace so great is magnified !

Welcome beneath our roof.　Art thou in
　　health ?

But thou awearied art : partake our fare ;

Refresh thyself with needful rest and sleep ;

Possess thy soul with care ; and may the GOD

Who of Zarephath's lonely widow not

Unmindful was, watch over thee for good.

　　To whom the Virgin mild, in sweet re-
　　sponse ;

Her fairest cheek, heart's index true, suffus'd,

Meanwhile foretelling, as dawn's blush the day,

For utt'rance, what emotions struggling there :—

　　Now more, if more might be, do I extol

His goodness, who my hope so well rewards;
Who, for my weakness, this assurance still
Hath added : that, naught questioning the
        means,
Thou should'st so straightly reckon of my
        state,
To every mortal ear, my lips unseal'd.
But with thine own, my spirit did rejoice
For thy good fortune, yet before mine eyes
Had brought it witness, or beheld it here
Itself to testify.   To thee, my heart
Hast'ning, hath led my impatient feet : with
        thee
Would I abide, gladly, now in this time
Of GOD's mysterious Hand; where to enjoy
Lov'd sympathy's pure flow, and counsel safe,
Thy often proofs of love give surety.
Much, much this full heart must to thee reveal:

But time of rest draws on ; and now fatigue,

Which naught I felt before, while eager thee

To embrace, comes o'er me : with the coming
    day,

With many days, prosper the LORD our ways,

Sweet shall be our communion.

                      Thus, in much joy

These holy women met and converse held ;

Brief, for scarce yet begun to mutual share

Their hearts' large store, ere to their rest
    retir'd :

For now, black night, in spangled darkness
    rob'd,

Driving her sable chariot thro' the air,

Shadow'd the earth in gloom ; and all their
    wants

Regarded, the saintly priest, with eyes upturn'd,

Speaking a speechless language, worshipful,

Struggling for utt'rance from his o'ercharg'd
        heart,
Commended all to GOD's protecting care.

    Soft fell of evening mild the golden glow
On Hebron's ancient walls ; soft on her
        heights,
Crown'd with their towers of white conspic-
        uous ;
Whence watchmen scann'd of old approaching
        foe,
Through dark defile or glen, and warning gave.
As perch'd on some bold cliff, or rugged spur
Of Anahuac, that o'erlooks wide round
Sonora's plains, and Gila's cañons stern,
The wild Apache, on his prairie steed,
With eagle plume, and feather'd lance at rest,
Scours with sharp sight the blue horizon 'round.

Now Mamre and the fruitful Eschol vied
In rich luxuriance of vernal charms;
For virgin Spring, by blushing Thallo led,
Fair bride, was just come forth in gay attire
To wed the joyous year; while woodland
    chant,
And zephyr soft, sung sweet their nuptial
    hymn.

There was a field hard by, whose borders
    lay
Within the slopes that clos'd Machpelah vale;
Where frequent at this time, Elizabeth
Forth walk'd from her foretime severe recluse,
And relaxation healthful sought. It stretch'd
Its verdant length across the vale, and seem'd
A very carpet spread of loveliness.
A brook of limpid water from the hills,

Tumbling with many a mimic fall, its course
O'er pebbly bottom held, bordering the field,
Cheering its way with rippling music wild.
At one extreme, some bold projecting rocks,
In natural structure pil'd, a cave had form'd ;—
The same the patriarch bought of Zohar's son,
Where still he sleeps:—whose portal was em-
        bower'd
With thickest growth of foliage : climbing rose
Of fragrant smell, with lichens mixed and moss,
And woodbine stout, aspiring over all.
Above, two stately palms their starry leaves,
Emblems of light, spread in perennial green.
Around, full many a shadowing tree, of oak
And terebinth and elm, and cypress dark,
Whose silent leaves unmov'd by passing winds,
Fit requiem for the noiseless grave rehears'd,
Shut out the view, and lov'd seclusion made ;

While nature's hand profuse its breast had
    deck'd

In flowery robes of variegated hue:

Sweet fern and lily, sage and violet bell,

Fennel, and thyme, and scented asphodel.

Earth nowhere offer'd a more lovely scene,

.To one endu'd with sensibility

To rural charms of sight or sound delightful:

Whose heart is open to the lessons taught

Of nature's simplest forms, as of her grand:

Who loves her in her rustic suit, as when

She puts her many-color'd garment on:

Who feels a spirit in the whisp'ring air,

As in the whirlwind's voice, when, furious

The forests o'er, he drives his lev'ling car:

Who sees a beauty in the humble grass

That clothes the verdant lawn, as in the cloud

By evening's mellow radiance gilded o'er.

More lovely not those storied vales, so oft
Of old in measured verse harmonious sung:
Nor Ghoutch, with its winding walks and
    groves,
Water'd by Chrysorrhoas' golden flood;
Nor Obolla's meads; nor that far Phrygian
    vale
Doganlu, nestled in its piney wolds,
Where wealthy Medas made his monument
And sepulcher: nor yet that sacred vale,
Where Salem's holy Priest the patriarch met,
Returning with the spoil of allied kings.

    Thither, upon this evening mild, withdrew
The Virgin and the matron: youth and age:
Like budding hope, by fruitful promise led.
Not new its quiet shades, its lov'd retreats,
Its walks, or charm'd beside the social stream
Ling'ring, or winding by the rocks retir'd.

Ofttime before, when childhood's gushing flood

Swell'd in her heart, to nature's promptings
true,

Here, as to her tribunal she had come,

And precious lessons learn'd: here play'd
beside

The brook, and pluck'd the lily from its bed :

And when to hilly Nazareth return'd,

Came many a childish memory stealing fond

Upon her melting hours; and then she walk'd

Anew its pleasant bounds; and paus'd to hear

The remember'd music of its stream; and
stoop'd

To pluck the lily, emblem of herself,

Knowing just where upon the margin moist

It grew, and how its virgin cheek it bent,

To receive chaste kisses from th' enamor'd tide.

This hallow'd spot, she said, how glad again

I view ! With each repeated visit, more
Its sacred haunts delightful; where my heart,
By fondest ties and tend'rest memories bound,
Turns ever true; where seems the very air,
With spirit of the saintly dead who here
In hope repose, as sanctified. How sweet
From out the fading west the mellow light
In chasten'd splendor falls !—gilding each tree,
And kissing soft the lifted cheek of bud
And flower and every humble thing, as if
To say good night ! Four seasons hath the
     vine
In triple yield its purple clusters dropp'd,
Since, then from childhood's dream just wake-
     ning,
With artless steps I rang'd these scenes among;
With simple heart their inspiration drew,
And thought no spot so fair: and now return'd,

Bids welcome each familiar scene again.

So may my heart, to Him who visits it

In love, bid gladly welcome His return;

So prove acceptable. But see, how o'er

Their tomb, the light in mild effulgence spreads,

As if an earnest of their hope! Thus hath

It ever faithful as God's promise shone,

Since long they slept; thus will till they in
    hope's

Fruition wake.

        As thus the Virgin spake,

O'er the flower'd green, their way, with linger-
    ing step

Pursuing; her fair face, as with the light

Divine of hope her own heart felt, illum'd;

Her full dark eyes. where beauty sat enthron'd,

Beaming with sympathy of nature's love,

Or in their spiritual gaze inspir'd, her soul's

Deep mysteries betraying: a bank they gain'd,

Projecting from the rocky base, with moss

O'ergrown, and blue-eyed daisies sprinkl'd,
    ting'd

With hue of shame, low shrinking in the
    grass.

O'erhanging boughs curtain'd it quite. The
    vale,

O'er which the eye, e'en to the far extreme

Wander'd uncheck'd, lay all outspread before.

Together, on this bank they sat; and, while

Fair Eos, goddess bright, still linger'd on

The tops oppos'd, ere yet with backward glance

Unto Tithonous' watery couch retir'd,

Whence, in love's rites her blushes all renew'd,

She rises at the dawn, with rosy smiles

To herald forth the day; admiring look'd,

A moment look'd admiring on the scene;

Communing

In look confiding, act, or answering smile.
Or palms' warm pressure, as they hand in hand
Were seated.

Yet spake no word meanwhile; their spirits
    pure.
Through silence, sweet interpreter, communing
    In look confiding, act, or answering smile,
Or palms' warm pressure, as they hand in hand
Were seated; Mary, humble, at the feet
Reclin'd of rev'rend age. Perhaps they thought,
As to the western main low sunk the king
Of day, in glory soon to re-appear,
Of Israël, benighted and forlorn;
To light whose wand'ring feet, to heal whose
    woes,
The Sun of Righteousness, more glorious King,
So soon shall rise. Howe'er it be, thus, soon
Elizabeth willing audience gain'd, and all
Of doubt dispell'd, what nearest to her heart.

How well beseemeth it, our mutual hearts

Should here in free communion be indulg'd
Of mutual thoughts, of mutual hopes and
    joys !
Here, where they rest in hope, to whom, fore-
    time,
The Promise was declared : looking to which,
They all have died ; which we to cherish, live ;
Thou, through infinite love to see fulfill'd.
To see fulfill'd ! yea, chosen of the LORD,
To whose fulfillment thou must minister !
O, who of Israël's daughters favor'd thus ?
    Whom Mary answer'd soon :—By so much
      more
My debt is magnified ; and all wherewith
To repay, is only love.   Ah, how enough
Extol His praise, His faithfulness declare !
Who found me lowly and hath rais'd me up ;
Meek, and with salvation beautified.

Soon as the heavenly summons came, that me
To this momentous service set apart ;
Though doubting not, though happy, all re-
    sign'd
To bow submissive to God's will, no rest
For peace remain'd, but in beholding thee,
And in thee witnessing persuasion's proof ;
The more, as of His favor certified
To theeward : condescending thus to aid
Inquiring faith, where comprehension fail'd.
And now, persuasion to assurance turn'd,
Comes longing to my heart, sighing to speak
Its bliss so full, its exercise so strange.
And where may confidence so sweetly flow,
Such fruits consoling yield, as here, with thee ?
    Mark'd her companion, pleas'd, the evident
       wish
Her mind to relieve, and thus, encouraging :—

Thou, in life's spring; I, in its autumn,
    walk :
And time, that points thee hopeful on, me
    beckons
To the vale of years. Gladly do I obey;
Knowing in whom my trust is plac'd, where
    wait
His rod and staff to aid my sinking steps.
But not without the fruits, so may I hope,
Of true obedience, pass'd my sojourn here :
And if in aught of counsel I might aid
Thy tenderer years, where trial sore must be,
Thy duty, and thy stainless name between;
Or sympathy, or kindred love, to serve
May enter welcome to thy breast, how pleas'd !
For hard, where shrinking chastity, alone,
Defenceless stands, 'neath this cold world's
    suspect.

She said: and gently forward bending, left
Upon her virgin brow affection's seal.
Not fairer glows through twilight's crimson
    mists
The evening star, than shone her eyes upturn'd,
Serene, through rising dews of answering love.
When thus Elizabeth renew'd discourse:—
   Ne'er can I pay the LORD in thanks, who
    hath
Rewarded me with honor for reproach,
And show'd me how await resign'd his time:
And when with thee, joy enter'd our abode,
Humility no fitting words could frame
Of gratitude, for so much added love.
But since, my mind its first tranquillity
Hath lost, regretful, in disturbing thoughts:
Knowing thy state, thee still betroth'd, nor yet
Thy marriage consummate. O, let not then

Thy pure heart marvel at my sense perplex'd,
Touching the truth, to me by Heaven reveal'd ;
But say, if so it please thee well, and naught
Forbid of sacred duty or command,
How may it be, through GOD's mysterious
    work,
My soul was taught to hail, my heart embrace
In thee, the Mother of th' expected King?

    Sweet relief to speak and tell thee all,
Kept treasur'd, jealous, in my secret soul,
To whom the LORD hath like remembrance
    shown,
To whom referr'd, as one divinely call'd
The same blest end to further : e'en with him
Unshar'd, tow'rd whom I no concealment know
Beside : and this my chiefest grief; to feel
I may not unto him, my dear betroth'd,
Who trusts in me, this mystery impart :

My apprehension this; when he the truth

Must know. O, not in man to comprehend

With woman's quicken'd sensibilities;

Less, to believe my state as wrought of God,

To nature opposite. But thou canst feel

The conflict how severe beneath whose weight

Must shrinking virtue sink, did she not lean

Upon an arm, Almighty to sustain.

My God, my cause, my good name will defend,

Than life more dear; all in His hands I leave.

She paus'd; as hesitating how her speech

To frame, where things supernal made the
    theme,

And trembling Innocence stood listening by

To hear her vindication; but assur'd,

Continued soon :

Not many times has run

Yon setting orb his round, since, in my prayers

At early hour engag'd, my face toward

Jerusalem, with tears I sought the LORD,

And spirit low abas'd ; and fervent plead

With supplicating voice, and strong desire,

For His returning smile to Israël :

That soon He would retake her by the hand,

And lead her from the darkness where she
　　　gropes ;

And soon, the mighty Prince to David's throne

Exalt, with judgment and with equity

Establish'd new.　And, while as thus I pray'd,

And meditated on the holy book,

And ponder'd, much perplex'd, and wonder'd
　　　much

As oft before, on those mysterious words,

Where, of the sign to Ahaz giv'n, 'tis writ :

A virgin shall conceive and bear a Son :

Image my great amaze ! when, quick as lights

Before me stood a glittering Shape divine

A sunbeam, silent as a shadow falls,

Before me stood a glittering Shape divine ;

Though not the splendor his, so terrible

In dazzling lustre bright, that prostrate strikes

With awe confounded, but that fascinates

The sense, and charms with love involuntary.

In kindly salutation his left hand

With winning gesture he extended : bore

His right a lily, that so graceful pois'd,

Seem'd e'en from his fair fingers forth to grow.

Surprise and wonder mix'd, possess'd my mind.

Alone, his presence all unheralded,

A something so majestic in his look,

A goodness so attractive in his smile,

His grace refin'd of mien, the gentle play

Subdued, of lambent glory on his cheeks,

And all with such celestial beauty crown'd,

Bade rev'rence own the origin divine,

And purity suppress alarm.   I stood

As one transfix'd, nor knowing in what sort

Reception to bestow; yet not in dread.

Speech had I none to question of his will.

With eyes down-cast, submissive, meek I stood,

His summons waiting on; till quite remov'd

Was   doubt, and   trouble vex'd my anxious
          mind,

As me saluting, thus, benign he spake.

   Hail, Mary! thou that highly favor'd art,

The LORD is with thee: bless'd among women
          thou.

And be not fearful, Mary, for with GOD

Great favor hast thou found.   Behold, a son

Thou shalt conceive and bear, and JESUS shalt

Thou call His Name.   Great shall Ho be, and
          Son

Of the Highest call'd : and GOD shall give to
    Him
His Father David's throne : and He shall reign
Over the house of Jacob evermore ;
And of His kingdom there shall be no end.
    Embolden'd then by these His gracious
    words :
How shall this be, seeing I know not man ?
Inquiring and amaz'd, I said : When, thus,
Full quick the kindly spirit deign'd reply.
    The Holy Ghost upon thee shall descend,
The power of the Highest shall o'ershadow
    thee :
Therefore shalt thou call that holy Thing
Which shall be born of thee, the Son of
    GOD.
And more attend ; thy cousin Elizabeth
Hath also in her age conceiv'd a son :

This the sixth month with her, who barren
    was :
For nothing is with GOD impossible.
    Then fill'd, for this assur'd felicity,
My soul with rapture inexpressible.
Yet did not humble resignation fail
To bow submissive to the Will supreme :
And all my bliss could find to answer, this :
    Behold the handmaid of the LORD : be it
To me according to thy word. So said ;
When quick the heavenly visitor withdrew,
With kindliest benedictions ; and in place, ·
Pressing their claims upon my o'erwrought
    sense,
Left hope, bliss, wonder, gratitude, amaze.
    Thus, have I all confess'd of word or act ;
And lighter beats my bosom. What remains
Thou knowest ; how to greet thee fond I sped

Anticipating. But thou didst not know
My exultation, when thy words inspir'd,
Cloth'd my rich blessing in the self-same form
The Angel used before : then the full blaze
Of evidence, like the mid-day sun, shone forth
Apparent. Then I deeply felt, our GOD
How faithful to His covenant. O, to feel
My Joseph knew as thou, as thou believ'd,
This joy were chang'd to ecstacy! She
    ceas'd :
But scarce, when rapturous thus her friend :
                         Now all
Is light ! The promis'd blessing is at hand,
And comes His Herald to proclaim His way!
Prepare His throne: exalt His glory high,
Who comes with judgment and with victory
    crown'd.
Arise, put on thy strength, O Israël !

And trust in Him who thy Deliv'rer comes,

Spread out thy wings, for peace inherits now,

Wide as thy borders, O Immanuel!

Now, all is light. And then the Angel said,

The Holy Ghost shall come upon thee! Thus

Do I embrace in thee the long'd-for Hope.

For thee and for thy care, leave all with GOD.

Commit thy cause to Him, who will approve

Thy purity undefil'd before the world,

And be thy sure defence. But see, the day

Is set.   Night's harbinger proclaims her ad
      vance,

And she draws on apace: and evening damps,

Distilling cool from humid bank and fen,

Advise retreat. To seeming, restless time

Hath tarried, pleas'd to listen to thy words.

Let us retire: and as we homeward walk,

If so thou dost desire, I will relate

How came the holy angel Gabriel,

To Zacharias in his prayers:—the same,

I deem, who to thee came; the pictures one

That paint his gracious presence and his voice;

Though then, than now more gloriously at-
 tir'd ;—

And what for unbelief befell. So did:

While Mary thoughtful heard and treasur'd
 much.

And while the sun o'er th' ecliptic course,

From his goal in watery Aries starting, ran

One quarter 'round upon his annual race,

The Virgin with Elizabeth abode:

Much wisdom from her long experience

Drawing the while; while she in her young
 love,

Felt life renew'd and zeal. Then was fulfill'd

Elizabeth's day of hope ; and all rejoic'd

In her rejoicing that a son was born.

And Mary sought her distant home : sore
tried

'Twixt apprehension and confiding trust.

She, fair young olive planted by the stream,

Its tender blossoms now unfolding first

To meet the frosts of life.   Reflecting sought :

And seem'd, in her so great solicitude,

Like virtue rous'd at foul suspicion's touch,

That shrinks within the soul's stern citadel,

In awful armor girt of innocence,

At thought of accusation.   Hard her task ;

Her trial sore : The faithful patriarch's less,

When, by command he lift his hand to slay

His only son, and yearn'd his bosom, wrung

At that so touching, tender, sweet appeal :

My father, lo, the fire ; but where the lamb ?

For, this, nought doubting GOD could wake
    again

From sleep, in figure saw his loss restor'd.

But she look'd up where none can wait in
    vain :

And needed much whereon her strength to
    stay.

Like some fair tendril lifting up its head

On bleak hillside, or in some shaded place

Where visits not the genial warming ray,

Expos'd to every chilling blast that blows,

Stretching its tender hands to find support

Whereon to cling embracing ; such was she.

For who would credit her report ? the truth

Who witness for her ?   Would the elders stern ?

Would Joseph, her betroth'd ?   Ah, this, o'er
    all

Her anxious heart distress'd, to see his grief,

To feel his scorn, who claim'd her inmost love.

If Joseph not believ'd, then all is lost;

And violated law its majesty

Asserts.   Death, frightful, claims its victim
      doom'd;

Dishonor, degradation railing point:

Impeach'd on justice' altar immolate'

The crown of woman's glory, chastity!

How be 't, to Nazareth she retraced her steps,

Bearing within her life the precious germ

Of Life and Light and Immortality.